TEN DOG TAILS

TEN DOG TAILS

Maggie Tellado

authorHOUSE®

AuthorHouse™
1663 Liberty Drive
Bloomington, IN 47403
www.authorhouse.com
Phone: 1-800-839-8640

First published by AuthorHouse   05/10/2011

ISBN: 978-1-4634-0643-1 (sc)
ISBN: 978-1-4634-2050-5 (ebk)

Library of Congress Control Number: 2011908204

Printed in the United States of America

Any people depicted in stock imagery provided by Thinkstock are models, and such images are being used for illustrative purposes only.
Certain stock imagery © Thinkstock.

This book is printed on acid-free paper.

CONTENTS

CONTENTS

DEDICATION

To the pets who have passed on and the owners who cherish them in their memories. If you love animals, adopt a shelter pet and those from breeders who really care about their animals and not just the money they bring. How desperately your love and care are needed . . . Give them a second chance and be their voice. Make a difference! If you can't treat an animal with love, don't own one.

"I'M NOT JUST A DOG"

by
Maggie Tellado

My **paws** are big or tiny,
My **teeth** are dull or shiny,
My **ears** are short or floppy,
My **mouth** is dry or sloppy,
My **eyes** are clear or teary,
My **coat** is short or hairy,
My **smile** is sweet, when I see a treat.
My **hope** is you'll remember whenever you feel
pain,
I **feel** the same thing too and try not to complain.
Your **care** is what I truly need,
Your **love** helps plant the daily seed,
Your **patience** keeps me safe and strong,
Your **guidance** helps my training along,
Your **kindness** leads the very way,
Your **smile** is always there to say,
You're **here** for me each and every day,
And **never** hurt me in any harmful way,
Your **trust** is a faithful promise I cherish above all
things,
I **love** you, my dearest friend,
I'll be with you till the very end.

CHAPTER ONE

KIRBY, THE RUNAWAY DOG

Hello there! I'm **Kirby**, a white male Peekapoo dog who lives on the East Coast with Ruth and Gino, my owners and my best friends who love and care for me. In their house, I feel like the King of the Castle and so proud to be here. **Sammie**, a black CockaPoo, who lives with their grandson Jimmy, visits me daily and boy do I like that! So, why don't you kick off your shoes and get comfy while I tell you my story of how I got here from the state of Alabama.

Gino's son and his family lived in Alabama and they had three dogs of their own and mated my mother with another friend's dog. Thus 64 days later, four pups were born, but only two survived. The whole family are dog lovers and one day Gino and a buddy of his went down to Alabama to visit his son and fell in love with the first litter of pups and was sad that two were lost. Gino wanted to take one pup home to the East Coast, but Ruth said "no." She got too attached to her pets and the issue

5

was then dropped. A year later, another litter of five pups was born at Gino's son in Alabama.

In the meantime, Gino got very sick and needed to have surgery for his heart (and he has a big one too, and kind). He recuperated well, but felt very depressed. Gino's son in Alabama suggested a new puppy would cheer Gino up and be good therapy too. Again, Ruth said "no."

When Gino felt better, months later, he went to Alabama with his friend to visit his son and saw the puppies, now almost ten weeks old and that is when I came into the picture. You guessed it! Gino came home with me. You see, I was so irresistible and still am. Ruth was very upset when she saw me with Gino in his car and gave him all responsibility for my care to him. Isn't she stubborn?

Gino took over and gave me so much love and I gave it back to him. We walked to help Gino's heart heal and get better and I really like that a lot. I don't care much for the collar, but Gino says it keeps me safe, so I don't fuss when he puts it on me anymore. Once in a while, Gino would catch Ruth petting me and he would smile. She's softening up, thank goodness!

As I was growing up, there were some accidents, but I was trained to go outside and stay off the furniture, especially that darn large Oriental rug in the center of the living room. Ruth trained me to only walk around the rug's perimeter on the hardwood floor. The rug was off limits to me. I tried once in a while to put my paw on it to test her, but boy did she get that broom out of the closet and pushed me off it. Since I really am a quick learner, I stayed off the rug because I didn't like the prickles of the broom pinching me.

But, Ruth did buy me lots of toys and goodie treats and treated me nice. She had this thing about dressing me up on holidays. Easter I was a rabbit, Christmas I wore a Santa suit and the Fourth of July I had to wear a red, white and blue banner with a hat. On Halloween, she went totally crazy. I did not like any of the outfits, but sure got a lot of attention and extra treats, so I went along with the program.

Anyhow, Gino and Ruth and their family would go away every year to celebrate three birthdays. One was Gino's, then Ruth's was three days later and their friend Lois was the same week. So, off they went to the Catskills every year in July for a week's vacation. I love to travel too, so I was happy I was going and Sammie was too. After all, we need companionship too.

Well, not so. Bad news for both of us. The plan was that I was going to stay with a relative, Aunt Mary and Sammie goes to the Vet. Oh, that's even worse! No, no, they can't do that to us. We have feelings too and want to go with them. The answer was a firm "no" and off I went to Aunt Mary's and her family. Even though I liked her and her family, I want to be with Gino.

Gino and Ruth dropped me off, happy as larks about their yearly vacation and patted me on the head.

"Don't go, I'll be mad if you do," I thought to myself.

All the barking and pouting didn't work and they drove off while I watched out the window, missing them already. One whole week, that's too long. It's like a hundred years. Aunt Mary gave me a new toy and she played with me and walked me a lot. There was a new chewy in my bowl and I didn't refuse it. (I'm not stupid, you know). That worked the first day.

The next day I moped around, looking out the living room bay window, then laid on the couch. Aunt Mary let me do almost anything, even walk on her rug. I rolled around on it and scratched my back. Every hour, I watched the cars go by, hoping Gino would pull up in the driveway. It was nerve racking watching so many cars go by. I think I counted twenty in a half hour and got so tired I took a nap. When I woke up, not only did I miss Gino, but Sammie and my house. I was alright with Ruth being gone to the Catskills, she was the one who got me to stay here with Aunt Mary. Bad Ruth!

Three days at Aunt Mary's and I was so lonesome for my family. So, I came up with a plan of my own. I would go and find them and we would all be back home together. One happy family!

DAY # 1: I waited for the side door to open and out I went running faster than a gazelle. No fence around the yard was great and I kept on going. Everyone came running after me and I still ran and didn't look back. I wanted Gino! A friend of Aunt Mary's who was a track star, chased me down the railroad tracks for about a mile until he cut his foot and lost his shoe. I outran him and kept on going.

Leaving them behind, I was on a mission to find Gino and rescue Sammie out of the vet's too. I've been running for a few hours and boy am I tired. It's getting dark and I can't find my family. Good thing it is summer time and not winter. My paws hurt from these stones and I need to rest for a while. I'll just lay down by this shady tree and start searching after a nap.

I woke up in the dark and it was scary. I miss my own bed and my toys and good food, but most of all, I miss Gino and reading the morning paper with him while I sit on the back of his neck. Hope he misses me too!

DAY # 2 was a long, hot day and the trail by the tracks seems endless. The noise of the trains scares me and I don't like it at all. Where is my family? I even miss Ruth now. Aunt Mary's husband and friends search for two days for me and could not find any trace of me. She got sick over my running away and I was really sorry. I was a bad dog, but I just missed my family so much. I think it's called "Separation Anxiety."

In the Catskills, the whole family was having a great time. While everyone was celebrating their birthdays, I was so lonely. However, the great time ended when Aunt Mary's husband phoned Gino and Ruth's son, Donnie, who was also there with them at the Catskills with his family. Donnie was told the news of my escape and was terrified I would be lost forever and poor Gino. Donnie could not let on about me and only told his wife Sherry. He had to make up an excuse to get back home and try to find me. As far as Gino and Ruth and the rest of the family knew, there was an emergency at his job and he was needed back home. Donnie was an important department head for the State Highway and in charge of a major project that needed him right away. Naturally, Gino and Ruth were upset Donnie had to leave on their birthdays, but he insisted he had to go. Donnie was really worried and feared for Gino.

DAY # 3: I was growing weary from traveling and the weather had turned from sunny, nice days to thunderstorms for almost a full day. I was never outside in a storm at home and was regretting I ever left Aunt Mary's house. The lightning and thunder scare me and I had to find shelter . . . somewhere. Gino's son, Donnie arrived home that evening after a five hour drive from the Catskills and went straight to Aunt Mary's house. There was still no trace of me and it looked bad. Aunt Mary was so upset, but it was not her fault at all. She was always good and nice to me. I was the one who chose to run away.

Back home now, Donnie and his friends made fliers and put them all around the area and also a photo of me (nice one, too) in the newspaper with a reward of $300. (Wow, I am really loved.) Hope someone finds me soon as I am very tired and want to go home. Where am I?

Donnie went on a three day search with flashlights, compass, food, and everything he could think of, determined to find me before Gino came back home from the vacation. So far, no luck!

DAY # 4—The storm finally stopped and the sun is shining again. I am so hungry and dirty and have these sticky things on my hair. I found a few pieces of food near the railroad tracks and drank some rainwater in a puddle. My chewies and food do taste a lot better and how I wish I had one now.

As I stop to rest again, I wonder, will I ever find Gino and Ruth? If there is a God for dogs, please bring me home to them. I'll never roam again.

DAY # 5—I'm really lost! The railroad tracks are endless. I am trying to rest as much as I can and my paws are ripping up from stones and small pieces of glass. Where is the end? Someone please come and find me.

Gino and Ruth are in the Catskills for one more day and then back home. Tomorrow they leave to come and pick me up and get Sammie from the vet. But, I won't be there at Aunt Mary's. Oh my! Donnie could not begin to think of how he would tell his father Gino about me. It will break his heart and maybe Ruth's too and little Ronnie who lives with Sammie. Day after day, Donnie and friends still continue searching surrounding towns and put up more fliers, but so far, no one has answered the ads. It was looking very bleak for me to be found.

DAY # 6—Exhaustion has set in and I have slowed down a bit. I found more food, a half eaten burger and some fries in a crumpled up McDonald's bag. Water is still available and I drink a lot of it whenever I'm thirsty, which is very often. It's getting hotter now, even during the daytime and I look for shade to rest. This was the biggest mistake of my dog life and wish I could take it all back. I don't remember how to get back to Aunt Mary's house since I never traveled alone before. My spirits are low and I lick my paws a lot to ease the pain of the cuts and try to bite off these sticky things on me, but they hurt my mouth.

The fearful day of Gino and Ruth's return was here and Donnie was beside himself with worry and how to break the sad news to his parents. Sammie is lucky, he will be going home today, not me. Gino and Ruth arrived at Aunt Mary's and Donnie was also there when they walked in the front door. The look on their faces was not a happy one. After he welcomed his parents back home, Donnie said he had something to tell them and to sit down. Gino asked where I was and called out my name. Aunt Mary and her husband left the room.

Donnie's voice was shaking as he started to speak. He told Gino and Ruth how I ran out the side door and all the awful details of the last six days of searching for me, putting out fliers, photos and with no luck. They had done everything possible. Everyone broke down in tears over me, even Ruth. Aunt Mary returned to the living room and told Gino how sorry she was I was gone. Gino knew it was not her fault and told her so. It was the saddest day of their lives, and mine too.

For the next two days, Gino could not eat or sleep. He cried for his Kirby and everyone wondered where could I be? Nothing was left to do, except pray.

DAY # 7—One week later, when all hope was just about gone, Ruth got a phone call while making dinner and it was a man's voice. She thought it was a crank call due to other calls they had received. (That was cruel to do.) The man spoke to her and convinced Ruth by identifying the tag on my collar. He had seen me in front of a 7-ll store from across the road, near the tracks. The glimmer of my tag shining in the sun called his attention to me. The man came over to me and gave me some cool, fresh water from his bottle and something to eat. He is a nice man and I am so happy someone found me, at last!

Ruth cried out for Gino, who was in the garage, listening to 50's music. Gino ran inside and saw Ruth on the phone. She told Gino, with happy tears, that the nice man on the phone found me and was with me at the 7-11 store. He saw the flier posted there and phoned them. Gino took the phone from Ruth in his shaking hand and arranged to meet the nice man in one hour. Yes, please come and get me, Gino! Only, I did not know I would see my family very soon, but was happy the man gave me water and food and petted me too. He even poured water over my sore paws, it felt good.

My whole family got into Gino's car and drove to meet the man who saved me. The happy reunion took place in a parking lot eight miles from where Aunt Mary's house was. I had traveled that far, for seven days, trying to find my family, only to almost lose them. I have learned my lesson in the darkest hour of my life, you can be sure of that.

The moment I saw Gino get out of his car, I knew it was going to be alright. Gino's tears of joy covered my face and it was the best feeling in the whole world. I even saw Ruth crying and knew she really loved me too. Finally, I was back with my wonderful family and knew how lucky I was and thanked the God for dogs for bringing me home.

That night, after a warm bath and brushing those stickers out, I felt so peaceful. I ate a little and drank lots of water and saw a new chewy in my bowl and a new toy in my bed. But, Gino picked me up and put me in bed next to him and hugged me for the longest time. Ruth came in the bedroom and sat by our sides, petting me for a few moments and kissed Gino goodnight. She thanked God for my happy return and to see the joy in Gino's face once again. The next day they took me to the vet for a complete check up. Sammie was there and came running over to see me and I could have done flips for being so happy. The vet said I was dehydrated and lost a few pounds, but under the circumstances of my story, I would recover nicely. I guess the vet is not so bad and maybe that was my lesson to learn.

Life was good again and I am thankful to the man who rescued me and cared enough to find my owners. I am home for good and no more roaming. Just to make sure, Gino and Ruth now send me to the vet with Sammie during their vacation week at the Catskills. I don't mind anymore and feel safe there and know my family will come back to get me. I'll love them furever!

More tails to follow . . . .

CHAPTER TWO

MIMSEY AND ME, THE YORKIES

Woof! It's **Toby** here. I live in Florida with Janice and Philip and that little sister of mine, **Mimsey**. I was born in Argentina and moved to Florida when I was six months old. I'm a male Australian Silky Yorkie and good looking, I'd say. The minute I looked at Philip and Janice, I knew I would be going to a good home and hoped for lots of room to run. There isn't much room in the cage at the pet shop and can't wait until they let me out to run around.

Gee, was I ever happy when I saw the big house and the big rooms inside. I feel like the Top Dog of the street and I was even happier when I first met Grandma Mimi, who lives with Philip and Janice and made a big fuss over me. Grandma Mimi would sneak some table food in her hands at dinner time thinking Janice did not see. Sometimes Janice did and would say something, other times she kept quiet and smiled to herself.

This wonderful family watches over me carefully, but one day I got into trouble by investigating my new neighborhood and got caught under the fence with my head. Luckily, Janice was there and pulled me out, very gently. What was I thinking? When I grew a little older, I had some problems with my tummy and it worried Philip and Janice, but the medication helped and I am better.

My favorite toy is the first one Janice's best friend Christy bought for me. It was an orange bone and then a little duck. I played with it so much, it's worn, but I still like it. My other two favorites are Nemo and the Big Yellow Chicken, who dances to the Chicken Dance. He's really funny and lights up when he dances, but he's too big and heavy to carry around, I tried it, so I know. I didn't like the toy with the tail and the ball that rolls around the floor. I can't catch it. It's frustrating!

Grandma Mimi would laugh and smile watching me play with it. I really like it when Philip and Janice took me in the SUV to pick Christy up from the airport. I always knew when it was "Car Time" since I am a smart little guy.

When I am outside in my yard, I want to do my business in privacy. It took a while, but I trained Janice not to look at me when I have to go. She will hide her eyes in her hands and then I feel more relaxed and private. If she tries to peek through her fingers, I stop. She knows my routine and we do the eye and finger hiding thing every time I go outside now. She was easy to train!

Night time and television time are my favorite times because I would sit between Philip and Janice and fall asleep. Sometimes, I would go over to Grandma Mimi and sit on her lap. When I get tired and want to go to bed, I would "woof" at Janice, only one time, around 10:00 p.m. It was my signal to her saying, "let's go to bed." Janice then picks me up and off we go to the bedroom to watch more t-v together until I fell asleep or if Philip came to bed. Janice caught on quick with only one "woof." I still do it to this day and think I really am a smart dog.

Daytime we all take a nap for two hours and then I get up and play outside after I do my business. (Don't watch me, Janice. I see you peeking!) In March last year, I got very sad when Grandma Mimi got sick and went to heaven. I miss her a lot!

Well, my life is good and I was very happy. Yet I don't know why, but I think Philip wanted to make Janice happy after Grandma Mimi left us, so one day they went to a pet shop and Janice saw this cute puppy, (not cuter than me, I hope) in the window and she wanted her. So Philip said "yes."

MIMSEY ENTERS

So here is why I had a life changing experience and it still goes on to this day. In walked Janice and Philip with this eight week old Australian Sydney Yorkie. She came from a private breeder in North Carolina. (Humm, a southern belle?) I didn't like her and she was a little spitfire from the first day she came to our home. Yeah, she's kind of cute, but had large ears and looked like Gizmo from the movie, Gremlins. I'm sure I am better looking. They named her "Mimsey" after Grandma Mimi.

Janice and Philip introduced us and I knew she was trouble. They tried to share their love with both of us, but that Mimsey would bite my ears and took all my toys, even if we had the same toys. Sometimes, she would walk underneath me at the same time I was walking and we looked stuck together like a magnet. It was funny to Philip and Janice.

Now listen folks, you know how it is. I had no privacy with this little terror in our house. She was at me, on top of me, under me and all over me most of the time. I almost hoped they would take her back to the pet shop and get a turtle or a fish. But not so, Mimsey was in for the long haul. That female canine chewed up Janice's pillow, her shoes and shoe straps, my toys, the edge of the dresser and our couch, on **my** side. She's a menace!

Mimsey went to sleep in her crate, but now her dog bed is next to Philip and Janice's bed, on **my** side. Luckily, I sleep on the bed, which she can't reach, yet. Good! When she is outside, Mimsey eats sticks, branches, rocks, lizard poop and one time, swallowed a bee that was in the grass. She found it and it stung her. We saw her shaking her head and licking her tongue. I don't do those things, I'm good.

Yet, one thing we do have in common is we don't like the mailman and the lawn guy. We go into spasms of barking when they are within an inch of our house and sometimes I even show my teeth (nice and pearly white, aren't they?) The neighbor next door moved and Mimsey and I can no longer

TEN DOG TAILS

intimidate the big rottweiler that used to live there.
(was it us?)

Now, it's a tiny little dog that lives there and goes
inside when we come out. That's no fun.

When Mimsey was about six months old, she
and I got into a lot of fights. I mean real fights.
When I would sit by Philip and Mimsey would sit
by Janice, the minute we looked at each other,
the teeth showed, we growled and then lunged
across at one another to fight. We meant business!
I didn't want her by Janice and she didn't want me
by Philip. Even when they changed partners, we
still did the same thing. Let's face it. We're jealous.
Janice did get Mimsey fixed, which helped a little,
but not much, maybe for a week or so.

Philip and Janice didn't know what to do with
us. (I did! Get rid of Mimsey, but they never asked
me). Philip came up with the idea of an "Educational
Tool." It was a yardstick he would tap on the floor
to get our attention and distract us. It worked for a
short while, until we got the hang of it. We knew he
would never use it on us. Poor Philip and Janice had
their hands full with us, but were intent on finding a
common ground. A friend of theirs suggested a dog
trainer. (What's that, I thought? A dog psychiatrist?)
No sir, I'm not jumping through any hoops or
dancing in a circle with a skirt on. Let Mimsey do it.
She's the trouble maker!

Okay, so here comes this lady trainer to our
house every Monday for one hour. It's obvious that
Mimsey needs the discipline and I am going to hold
my ground since I was here first. She's second. I
liked the lady dog trainer because it was mostly

about my sister's behavior. The problem was found out that Mimsey wanted to be the Alpha dog and I was not going to let her. There it is in a nutshell! The only thing we did not fight over was our food, strangely enough. Usually that is the opposite case. Janice feeds us in separate areas of the kitchen and we never take each others food. Thank goodness for that!

The dog trainer tried several things, such as direct eye contact from Philip and Janice to us when we started growling. It helped a little, but not completely. Next, she tried putting Mimsey's leash under the coffee table leg, away from the sofas where she could not jump up. Mimsey had to stay down on the floor and I stayed on the sofa, with Philip and Janice. Yippee! Mimsey would cry and whine and it made Janice and Philip feel bad. I even felt sorry for her and would jump off the sofa and lay down next to her. Go figure!

After a month of dog training, it was decided that the problem was Mimsey wanted to be the boss. The lady trainer left and we got a little better, but still got into some tiffs. It was constant day and night work for Philip and Janice and they were exhausted from the training guides they had to follow diligently. I am growing to like Mimsey, but she will have to realize I am the Alpha dog. Till then, we will still get into spats. Janice even put Mimsey in the dog carriage and took her for special walks alone, leaving Philip with me. She is just so spoiled and that's that. I, of course, will always be first since I came first. But I know they love us both the same.

When Mimsey does get too much attention, I lick the floor and don't know why.

The latest incident with Mimsey happened when she ate a green crayon when Janice bought a box for her nephew's little girl for her birthday and a coloring book too. Each day with her is a new experience and I wonder what will happen tomorrow. In a way, it's kind of exciting to see what she will do. Janice and Philip take us in the SUV a lot to visit their daughter Shelly and her family. Yikes, she has two dogs we don't get along with and it is chaos when we go there. Mimsey and I just like to be in our house with our stuff. So now when they visit Shelly, Aunt Barbara comes over to stay with us and watch us. We like her too!

Some new items have to be used to help our rivalry like a water gun, an air horn (which Mimsey wants) and the educational tool. She recently ate a caterpillar and sun bathes in the yard and can box on her hind legs and takes a power nap at 9:30 a.m. daily. I feel like a guard dog at times, watching her every move. She doesn't want me to have any attention, it's all about Mimsey. Janice gives us treats like sardines and chicken and we get to lick the ice cream bowl, our favorite treat.

I am happy to have Janice and Philip and the home they brought me to, and although Mimsey does wear me out, through it all she's still my little sister and I do love her. We are now at the point we can lay next to one another and relax. It's been a long, hard road, but she's here to stay!

More tails . . . .

CHAPTER THREE

WILLIE AND BRADY, SERVICE HEARING DOGS

Our owners are Denise and Gary, both hearing impaired and I am their Border Collie **Brady,** who will tell you our story. I was born on Halloween in California and at nine weeks old was adopted by my owners from a private breeder as a companion for their twelve year old daughter. Denise had applied for a service hearing dog before they got me, but the agency said there were too many applicants and to apply at another time. Denise was told I was too big due to other disabilities she had. Denise then went to a third service dog agency that specifically had smaller dogs but the agency folded.

Gary was working for the Parks Department and the cost of living in California was not doing well. So, he came to Montana, where we now live, to look for work. Denise stayed back in California to sell our house, but it took longer than they expected, but eventually it sold. Denise packed up our belongings and had movers ship them to Montana. We were on our way to be with Gary and our new home. Their daughter stayed in Montana to go to college.

During Gary's time away from us, I got lonely without him and wanted to be a family again. Denise and I could not wait to see our new home and meet new friends. Yeah! We're here and I like it. Yup! A few weeks passed and I was still lonely, so Gary went to a puppy rescue and fell head over heals for my brother they named **Willie**. Denise had no idea Willie would be joining our family, but Gary was not about to take him back by no means. Willie is a white husky mix and was born in Montana in the winter. At eight weeks old, Willie was our new and welcomed addition to our family and was a real good looker. Gary told Denise he rescued Willie for a companion for himself. (Nice try, Gary!)

The initial meeting of Willie and I did not go as well as my owners expected. In fact, we went nose to nose and snapped at each other until Denise and Gary tapped us on the nose to be nice. We then sniffed one another and soon we began to play and bonded very quickly in a couple weeks.

Denise was born hearing impaired and Gary lost all hearing in his right ear at the age of twelve due to a football injury. Both of them read lips too! Our family got settled in Montana and opened a small business. One afternoon, a customer came to the store with a service dog. Denise found out from the customer that she could train her own dog as a service hearing dog, so Denise bought the Guide Book on how to do it.

Another time, while at their store, Denise happened to meet another woman named Gloria, who saw the Guide Book Denise was reading. They talked and Gloria told Denise she rescued animals and was a trainer also and offered to help train Brady, in exchange for Sign Language lessons. The Guide Book stated that two people were needed for dog training in the beginning.

During my training time, it was Willie who was used as the distraction for my focusing. Soon, Willie learned the commands as well and after six months, Denise had to train both dogs on her own while Gary ran the store. Both Willie and I passed the Basic Training and are now Service Hearing dogs. Did you know there are several different kinds of service dogs. Here are the categories: **Hearing service** dog, which is an assistance dog specifically selected and trained to assist people who are hearing impaired (like Denise and Gary) by alerting their handler to important sounds, such as doorbells, smoke alarms, ringing telephones or alarm clocks. We can also work outside the home, alerting to such sounds as sirens, forklifts and a person calling the handler's name. We are tested for proper temperament, sound reactivity and willingness to work.

Another type of service dog is the **Autism service dog, Guide dog, Medical Response dog, Mobility assistance dog, Seizure response dog, Service dog, Assistance dog, Psychiatric service dog and Emotional Support animal.** I'll bet you didn't know there were so many.

Me, Brady—I am the more serious dog and feel happiest when I am working for Denise. I like car rides and keeping Denise alert and safe. I'm not much for toys, but goodies are great. Willie is more playful, but he will work and his favorite thing next to working is eating home made peanut butter snacks that Denise makes. They are used as a "Motivational Treat" for us.

Our yard is fenced in and there are many signs posted on the fence for people and kids to see. We do like people, but when they come near our domain, we turn into Jekyll and Hyde and look at the kitchen window to see if Denise is watching. When she comes outside, we freeze and look so innocent. At that point, we know we had better behave.

Rock Hunting in the mountains with Gary and Denise is a happy time for Willie and me. Willie hopes to see rabbits and bounces like one, imitating the rabbit, then chases them until the command of "leave it" is said by my owners. Then Willie stops. Usually, I like to chase after Willie and play along.

At home, tired and happy, we sleep in our big dog beds by Denise and Gary. During the middle of the night, I get up and do a house check, then check Denise and Gary. It's part of my job.

I am now eight years old and Willie is five. We are inseparable and the best of buddies!

Denise and Gary's choice in choosing Willie and me was a great one and they say we enrich their lives more than we know. They tell us we are valued above anything else and we are their ears and their "life line," giving them their independence. Willie and I thank them for the home and love they give back to us. It's great to be in their family!

More tails . . . .

CHAPTER FOUR

SKIPPY MC RUFF, THE DIABETIC DOG

Hello there! I'm **Skippy McRuff**, a toy Maltese dog from Pennsylvania who loves the snow and running around on our acre of land. The first time I saw the snow was when my owner, Petey and our exchange student form Brazil, Arturo, took me outside to train me. I was only eight weeks old and tried to lift my little leg, (I'm told that's what us males are supposed to do). I fell over into the snow since my balance was not nearly perfected, so I squatted down and did a good job. My owners were proud of me and so was I.

We live in a wooded community with lots of space to walk and are away from the noisy streets. I don't like them much, quiet is better for me. The deer come on our property all the time and they are fun to watch. A mother deer and her babies stayed by our house for a couple hours and I liked watching them through the back patio doors. A few times, black bears come up to our house and patio and try to eat the garbage. One time, I heard the bear and barked until Petey and Madge woke up. That bear sure looked hungry and mean.

Kayla, my Maltese sister, lives here with us and we get along just great. Our favorite room in our house is the family room with skylights and special places for our plush dog beds and if we feel like, we have our own lounge chair right next to the heat. Kayla and I cuddle up together in it when the weather is cold and watch the snow fall on the skylights.

In the summer months, Petey puts me in the wheel barrel for a ride when he does yard work. Kayla doesn't go in it—she's afraid of the wheel barrel. A funny thing happened one day during the fall season with Kayla. It was a Saturday morning and she spotted a deer in our yard. Kayla ran across the road and we didn't see her after that. One minute she was there, the next she was out of sight. It seems that the grass was so high and she fell right into a ditch near the grass. Next minute, here comes Kayla out of the high grass, shaking her head and looking dazzled. Poor Kayla! She stayed right near us the rest of the day and never ran across the street again, even if she saw the deers. She may not have thought so, but it was so funny as we saw her disappear, then jump out of the ditch.

In the spring, Petey and Madge sold our house and we moved to this warm place called Florida. Boy was it ever hot there and the drive was long and we slept a lot, except when we woke up to get gas or stay in a motel. The rooms we stayed in were all nice and roomy and had big beds. One for Petey and me and the other for Madge and Kayla. We could all stretch out after the long day's drive.

Finally, we got to our new apartment in Florida and Kayla and I sniffed around, trying to see if we would like it here. It was alright, but we missed our big house in Pennsylvania and the open spaces of land we owned. One good thing is that we had to be walked (on a leash, of course) and got to see a lot of different things and people.

I got curious one day at one of the rest stops in Florida when Petey walked me. I started rubbing my nose with my paw because my nose was hurting so much. When I looked down on the ground, I was standing on top of a mountain of fire ants (red ants) and when I went to sniff it, they starting biting me and I was sneezing and trying to snort them out. Petey saw what was happening and stomped on the red ants and took me away and washed out my nose. He got some on his pants leg and shoes too. It was very scary and hurt a lot.

Now my sister Kayla, who is as curious as I am, loves to chase geckos, those little green lizard things with a tail. Sometimes she catches them and they are then missing a tail. Kayla can spot one quicker than you can say the word "gecko." Another time on one of our walks, Petey and Madge saw a Bofu frog come right across our path. We got out of the way real fast. Bofu frogs are here in Florida and are very dangerous to pets, especially small dogs. They are brown and ugly and have two sacks on the side of their heads. They will attack dogs or cats by emitting the poison from those two sacks. If you don't flush out the poison immediately, with water to the side of the pet's mouth, not down the throat, they can die within minutes. The Bofu frogs usually hide in the grass after the rain and are hard to see. (Maybe the bears in Pennsylvania were better to deal with since they are so big and we can see them.) Now we are very careful when we walk and look around for the Bofu frogs.

Our new apartment has a lot of big windows and patios. I love them because I can see so much and Madge puts me and Kayla out on the patio every day, except when it storms. The storms here in Florida are bad and so is the lightning. We are afraid of them! Also, we have to go somewhere when this big storm, called a hurricane comes and trees and houses are destroyed.

Kayla's and my favorite place in the whole world was our trip with Petey and Madge to Disney World. We got to stay in a very nice hotel room and got fed special treats and met other dogs and their owners. It was the best time! Petey and Madge walked us so much around the hotel before they went on their outings, that we slept like newborn puppies. They even bought us our own dog bowls as souvenirs and two plush Pluto toys. Kayla tries to get the squeakers out and I am good and leave mine alone. She knows better than to come near my Pluto. Grrrr!

We have family sing-a-longs in our house. Petey taught us to howl when he sings and plays his guitar and although it's very cute, it drives Madge crazy. Once we get started, we don't want to stop. (Any movie agents out there? We're for hire.)

Kayla is very smart, but not as smart as me. She plays coyly and ignores Petey when he talks to her, but her tail wags the whole time. She hears him, but doesn't respond. Petey and Madge think it's funny when she does that. I don't.

The apartment was not roomy enough, so we moved to a new house in Florida with lots of room, just like the one in Pennsylvania and a huge fenced in yard, (but, watch out for those Bofu frogs.) We have no carpets in our house, only marble floors and it feels nice and cool when we lay on them. Kayla and I love to run and catch our toys as we slide on the floors. Sometimes we don't stop in time. Madge spoils us so much and we have dog beds in every room of our house, totaling ten beds.

So, here is how this story ends . . . . On another trip back to Disney World a year later, Kayla got pregnant and two months later I was the proud papa of four puppies, two boys and two girls. However, the timing was not good. Kayla had to have Cesarean section during a hurricane and the puppies were born at 4:00 a.m., in the vet's office, with Petey assisting him. Poor baby! I felt so sorry for her, since I was the one who caused her to get pregnant.

She forgave me and all turned out well. The puppies survived and so did Kayla. Petey and Madge adored my little off springs and Kayla was a great mom. Three puppies went to good homes when they were ten weeks old and everything turned back to normal and we kept one, the smallest one. Petey named her Baby Love. She was the one he delivered during the hurricane.

When I turned seven years old, I had a seizure and more of them after that. It really scared me and my owners and I lost my friendship with Kayla because I was so tired all the time from the medicine I had to take every day. I'm almost eleven years old now and have been a diabetic for over four years. I gained a lot of weight during these years from the medicine and have to get blood tests twice or more every year to check my diabetes. This last year we were able to lower my medicine from four to two types of medicine. I am frisky again and not so tired, but do take my naps. I can play with Kayla and Baby Love and walk outside. I am loosing my eyesight due to cataracts and the vet says I am three quarters blind. I know the inside of my house very well and where my beds and bowls are and my favorite place which is next to Madge's side of the bed. I bark when Kayla and Baby Love bark, but I can't see what or who I am barking about. I am the man of the house and have to protect my family. It is very frustrating to be this way—I wish I could see like my other friends. When it's time for my insulin, Madge is very gentle with me. She talks to me when I get my shots, twice a day, and gives me treats afterward. Sometimes the needles hurt and I know when my insulin is coming because I hear Madge when she opens the cap of the needle. I get excited and bark because I know it will make me feel better. After a while, I take my morning nap and dream of beautiful colors I wish I could see. Petey is good to me too, he gives me steak and shrimp when he has to give me the shots. When I get a seizure, it is very scary. I lose my balance and I start pawing, like I'm running and I can't move or walk. I'm in a different and scary world at that time. Madge can't help me while I'm having a seizure. She has to wait until it's over and then I'm very exhausted

When I can't see any more, I will be sad. I know with Madge and Petey's love and care, I'll be in good hands. I listen to their voices to guide me when I get confused. But, I'm still a lucky fella to have such wonderful owners and I trust them with my life!

A Short tail to follow . . . .

CHAPTER FIVE

THE FOLEY CLAN

We have to be the luckiest pets here in the state of Arizona. I'm **Zena**, an eight year old pug and here's my story.

I live with Sandy and Tim, our owners and friends and their three other pets. Sandy got me as a puppy from her daughter who moved out of state and couldn't take me. I fit in this "Clan," as I call it, like a pea in a pod. It's perfect here!

My favorite playmate out of the all the pets is **Amanda**, a three year old bulldog, who taught me some neat things. One was this . . . Tim, my owner, likes to eat his food with his plate on his lap, watching t-v in our living room. (Not to Sandy's liking, I'm told.) Well anyhow, Amanda would watch Tim prepare his plate and get ready to eat his food. Amanda would sit next to him on the sofa, almost on top of him and would whine and whine when he ignored her. When Tim does not respond to her whining, Amanda makes it louder and grunts. Then, when she's tired of being ignored, Amanda would sneeze on Tim's plate. He would push her away and she crept closer, whining again and continues her sneezing until Tim gives her a morsel of his food, (meat only, please.)

At first, when these gimmicks of Amanda's began, Tim would empty his sneezed on plate of food, but after so many times, he gave up and goes on eating his food and Amanda gets her way and a piece of meat. Tim really loved Amanda, but she was Sandy's girl from the time they got her. So folks, that's what Amanda taught me to do, sitting side by side watching and waiting for Tim's food to arrive. You see, it is Tim's fault for not sitting at the table to eat where we can't see the food or reach him. I think he just got used to our tradition and I carry it on every day at dinner time at 7:00 p.m. For some reason, Tim is the only one I torment with my sneezing. It's a fight to the end with me the winner.

Sadly, our Amanda passed away when she was ten years old and we miss her so much.

The other two pets that live with us are **Rocky**, a seven year old rescued boxer and **Nessa**, a four month old Collie. Rocky is a proud, regal dog who watches our house inside and outside. He became very lonely and wouldn't eat when Amanda passed on. Nessa was bought in Nebraska from a breeder when she was three months old and she blends in our family really well. Tim and Sandy drove to get her from Arizona to Nebraska and she loved the ride in the car and going outside. It was love at first sight between them.

Although Nessa, (her name is derived from an Irish name), is only four months old, Rocky taught her how to climb the fifteen stairs to the upstairs bedroom. They are very steep, but Nessa learned very quickly. I think she's going to be very smart, like me!

Now it's a game of stairs every day with Nessa and Rocky and one more thing she can add to her list of achievements. We are one, big, happy family at the Foley house and are cared for very well by our owners.

Sandy and Tim's three year old grand daughter, Maddie and her older brother Aiden, six years old and baby sister, Lexa, six months, just love their dog, **Max**. Max is a two year old Corgi and very frisky. He was a gift from their mom, Candee and dad, Sonny. I think all children should have a pet, don't you? They need to learn love and caring and responsibility, which helps them to have a good character as they grow up.

Anyway, I don't know how three year old's think, but one day, while Candee was washing dishes and Maddie and Lexa were in the next room where Maddie was coloring and very quiet, indeed. Candee peeked over once in a while to check on the kids and went back to cooking eggs for breakfast for them. When she was done cooking and called Maddie to the table, and went to get Lexa out of her swing, Candee got the surprise of her life.

The reason it got so quiet earlier was that Maddie decided that Max's white spots needed some color, so she filled in the white spots with the blue marker. (A future artist, maybe??) That wasn't enough coloring for her, so she went over to baby Lexa and colored the top of her head, blue. My, oh my! All I can say is that Max really had the blues that day! Thank goodness the marker was washable and so were Max and baby Lexa. Candee should have taken a photo of them, it would be a winner.

So, now Candee and Sonny have some funny stories to tell their kids when they grow up. I'm sure that's not the end of it and there's more to come. I can't wait! Bye for now.

More tails . . . .

CHAPTER SIX

HARRY AND THE POOL TABLE

I'm sitting here in the front seat of my owner Kate's 2004 Sonic Blue Mustang G.T., on our way to the dog park. I always feel like a celebrity when we go riding. First, we have to wait for Kate's grandson, Derek, to get out of school and I really like him. Kate just got divorced and she's not so lonely any more since I came to live with her. We live in the state of Iowa.

My name is **Harry** and I am part long hair chihuahua and terrier mix and just turned eight months old. I'm really good looking if I say so myself! My chest and paws are white and the rest of me is tan. We live in a big house with our relatives and have the whole downstairs to ourselves. It's very roomy and nice down there and private too.

I have a different story to tell of how I came to live with Kate. (And boy am I happy I did.) I'll start from the very beginning . . .

A stranger lady took my dad to a store in a mini mall and was going to tie him up and leave him there for anyone to take him. (Isn't that awful? What if he got loose? What if a bad person took him?

Bad Lady!!) Another nice lady saw that my dad was about to be left there all alone and she took him home with her. So, my dad was rescued that day and went to a good home. Yeah! The nice woman had another female dog at her home and three puppies were born two years later and I was one of them.

Kate's married daughter Polly, felt sad about Kate's divorce and wanted to make her feel happy and not feel so lonely. Polly likes garage sales and one day decided to go to one and saw the three puppies who were at the garage sale house of the nice woman. The woman told Polly the story of my dad and how she rescued him and now had three puppies. Polly wanted one of the pups for Kate and asked how big they would get. The woman showed Polly my dad, who was looking out the front window. It was a good size dog for Kate and Polly got me free from the nice woman. She gave Polly everything for me, a pet carrier and toys, plus food and training pads too. (Wasn't that kind of her?) Since the nice garage sale woman worried about who would take the other two pups she had grown fond of, she kept one and gave the other puppy to a good family she knew.

Polly rushed home and phoned Kate at work and told her she now has a new boyfriend waiting for her. Kate knew it was a new dog. Me! I took to Kate like peanut butter and jelly and I am her little boyfriend and she's just great to me. I don't care too much yet for the dog parks since there are so many other dogs I don't know and sometimes I get scared since I am small. I do like Kate's car a lot, especially when we go to pick up Derek from school. Derek holds me in the car while Kate drives and I don't like when big trucks come alongside us. It's very noisy.

I'm so smart I know when Kate gets ready for work and it is when she starts to brush her teeth in the bathroom and then she goes and shuts off the computer. I always run and hide so she doesn't leave me. Kate has to chase me to catch me and she always does. It's like a game to me, but then it's crate time. I don't mind it too much since I was in one since I was eight weeks old.

My crate sits on top of the big pool table, where I watch Animal Planet. Kate leaves the t-v on for me so I won't be lonely. She's so loving, she knew what it meant to be lonely at one time, not now. When I get tired, I fall asleep, but when I hear the door open and I see Kate, I go bonkers! When she's home from work, I follow her all over the house. She always takes me out of the crate first thing and hugs me and gives me kisses. When she watches t-v later on in the day or night time and doesn't pay attention to me, I paw at her hair until she notices me. Smart huh? Then, when she does notice me, I curl up and lick her eyes and give her more doggie kisses. We are a perfect match.

When the weather gets very cold, I have to wear this plaid sweater that I don't really like. It goes over my head and as soon as I see the snow, I say, "oh boy, here comes that plaid sweater again." I feel like a preppy in college. (Hey, I remember Bruiser

Woods wore a sweater too in his movie.) Good thing I grew out of the thing. Next year, when I am bigger, I want to pick out my own sweater at Pets Mart. Maybe something with bones and toys on it, that's more me. No plaid, please!

At bedtime when I was a puppy, Kate would put my dog bed next to her head. Now, when Kate lies on her back, I curl up on her legs until it's time to go to sleep. When the t-v is off, I know it's our bed time. Sometimes in the middle of the night, I go under the covers and fall asleep there where it's nice and warm and near Kate.

This may sound strange, but I have a favorite time and it's when Kate takes out the lint remover to clean the chairs and sofa. But, I get angry when she uses it on the chairs and not on me. So, I roll over on my back and wait for her to rub my belly with the lint remover. I know it's weird, but I like It! And another thing I do is this little thing with the side of my mouth. It's as if something was stuck and I'm trying to get it off my mouth. Kate told me her own dad used to do the same thing. (Now I know I'm really related.)

Breakfast is a time I really look forward to like most dogs. But, this is different. Every morning, Kate has her coffee and Biscotti to start her day. She soaks the Biscotti in her coffee (with flavored cream) and bites off a couple pieces for me. I'm real happy after that treat. Don't get me wrong, that's not my regular diet—just an early morning treat. You see, I do have a two sided bowl and a water bowl. One side is for dry food and the other side is for wet food in case I don't know which one I want that day. Spoiled, yes indeed! I wouldn't want it any other way.

My very favorite play toy is an empty sixteen ounce water bottle. Kate takes off the lid and the paper and I like to hear the crackling noise it makes when I play with it. When it gets too smushed up, Kate gets another one for me.

I'm now eight months old and you know what's coming next. I'm going to be missing two bottom parts and feel less of a man, Oh no, don't do it, Kate!

Today, we are going over to Polly and Derek's house and I can't wait to see them. Sugar is my favorite. She is a Lab mix and then there's Lacy who was abused and is afraid of men, until Polly adopted her and met Ray and Derek. Violet is a Cocker Spaniel and so is Precious, her little puppy. Polly and her family really have good, kind hearts and I'm part of the family too. I guess I am special.

By the way, I just remembered to tell you about last Halloween. Kate dressed me up as a cop in this blue hat and blue shirt. I did not like the elastic under my chin to hold my hat on. Kate accidentally snapped it a couple times putting it on my head for about the third try. I would not hold still and thought it was not cute, but everyone else did. You can be sure I made the rounds on her camera wearing that cop hat and shirt. I can't wait to see what's in store for me next Halloween. Maybe I'll hide the new outfit under the bed when Kate isn't looking. Good idea, don't you think?

Well, I hear Kate coming home, so I have to go. I want to thank my Aunt Polly who saw me at the nice lady's garage sale and gave me to the best friend and owner a dog can have. We will always be together and I am happy to live my dog years with her . . . and her only.

More tails . . . .

CHAPTER SEVEN

HARLEY AND THE BOYS

Hey there! I'm **Harley**, a Beagle dog and I live in the state of Delaware with my other boys and my owners, Karla and Matt and Charlie. Karla is the one who rescued me when I was very small for Matt, her son who was six years old, for a family pet. Charlie is Karla's father and we all live together in a small house by the Delaware River where I learned how to swim with Karla.

I have a Harley dog jacket and headband that Karla puts on me and I think I look pretty cool. I also do some neat tricks with a cookie on my nose. Matt puts it there and I hold it until he tells me it's okay. Then I flip the cookie upside down and eat it. I am the hit of the family when I do that trick. But, the funniest thing I do is the "Meaty Bone Dance." (I taught myself, you know.) Karla or Charlie will give me a Meaty Bone for a treat and I don't eat it right away. I leave it on the rug and lift up my paws and dance around the meaty bone for a couple minutes. Then, when I'm done dancing, I'll pick it up and eat it all. It gets lots of laughs and I'm a big hit with Karla's friends.

I like sticks and run with them in my mouth in the back yard when Grandpa Charlie throws them to me to fetch. One time, when I picked up the big stick, it got impaled in the roof of my mouth and it hurt so bad. Grandpa Charlie pulled it out of my mouth and looked at the wound. It was a big hole in the roof of my mouth and he rinsed it out with water. It got better in a couple days, but it was hard to eat food, so I got soft food.

D.J.

I'm **D.J.,** a Golden Retriever who was rescued by Karla when I was eight weeks old. I'm one of four pets that live with her and my family. I feel I'm the head of the dog household since I'm the biggest, but I don't think my buddies agree with me. In fact, the spunkiest of the crew is Teddy, the teacup poodle. He's not afraid of anyone or anything and don't even think of going near his ball. It's so worn out, yet he still plays with it after all these years. Grandpa Charlie bought him other balls, but he won't play with them. He just wants the old worn out ball.

I'm a real good eater and one day Karla left a tub of butter on the table and it was just within my reach and it smelled good. Naturally, my instinct took over and while no one was looking, I gripped the tub of butter with my teeth, sat down under the table and ate most of it.

Minutes later, when Karla cleared off the kitchen table, she looked for the tub of butter and was baffled, until I came out from under the table with butter all over my nose and mouth. Karla did not scold me and said, "D.J. What did you do?" I put my head down, of course, and the next thing I saw was a hard roll being handed to me by Karla. I remember her saying to me, "Since you already ate the butter, how about a roll too?" I did eat it and let me tell you fellow dogs, I had the runs for the rest of the day and felt awful. My curious nature got the best of me and you would think I had learned my lesson. Not!

Around Valentine's Day a couple years ago, Karla got a box of chocolate and flowers from Troy, her boyfriend. Half of the candy was left in the nice red box and was on the dining room table. Boy, oh boy, did that smell so good. Yummy! Karla was in the shower and I just had to get closer and take a sniff of the candy. It smelled good. Since I'm pretty big, I wanted another sniff of it, so I jumped up on the dining room chair and pulled the box of candy toward me, watching out for Karla.

I had never smelled candy like this before and it smelled much better than canned or dry dog food. Why doesn't Karla give me some of that? Why is it just for people? Or is it? I'll just try one and see for myself what all this fuss is about.

Wow is this good! I ate one, two, three and couldn't stop and finished the rest of the box.

Uh, oh, here comes Karla and the candy box is now empty. What now?

"D.J., what did you do? Bad dog."

Karla hurried up and phoned our vet, (don't like him, he gives me shots). Now I know why Karla said Bad Dog. All dogs can't have chocolate because it makes them sick and they can die. Oh, no. I never knew that!

So, I found out the hard way when I went into convulsions soon after. Luckily I survived and this time, I did learn my lesson. Even though I still like the smell of chocolate, I won't go near it ever again. I guess I'm the dog that gets into trouble and there's always one in the family, so I hear.

When Grandpa Charlie was cleaning out his shed, he put all his tools and tool box in the yard and tied my harness to the tool box because our gate got blown down from a storm. He didn't want to lose me and kept me near him. He went inside to get something to drink and I wondered why I was outside, with a tool box next to me. So, I wanted to be by him and started dragging the forty pound tool box across the yard to the back door. Grandpa Charlie couldn't believe I did that. He took me off the tool box and put me inside, where I could watch him from the back door with my buddies. I'm trouble.

Now you will hear a story from my brother, Teddy . . . .

TEDDY

I'm **Teddy**, a four pound teacup poodle that was bought by Karla from a private lady breeder. I was only nine weeks old and a tiny thing. My Grandma came with Karla to get me and Karla was afraid to hold me I was so small. Grandma took me to the car and stayed at home with us until Karla felt comfortable enough to hold me the right way. It was mutual love from the start between me and Karla.

Grandma said I looked like a fur ball with tiny legs.

I love to play ball with Grandpa Charlie every day and he walks me around the school parking lot. He needs exercise for his lungs and I'm his walking pal. Do you know that I can understand a lot of words and can count to three with my paws. Matt taught me how to do that after months of training. My breed is very smart and we do train very easily.

Brushing me every day is what I really like. Karla cleans my teeth with this finger toothbrush and special doggie toothpaste, which I don't care for. She says my teeth are important and it has to be done. Also, I have gotten used to going to the groomers and smell really nice when I come home. At first, I was bad when Karla took me there to have my nails trimmed and get groomed. The groomer would refer to me as "Freshy Boy." Now she likes me a lot and I like her.

I traveled with D.J. and Harley to visit Grandma in South Carolina. The drive took forever and we were very happy when we came back home. I really like my brothers, D.J., Harley, Tomas and Grandpa Charlie most of all, next to Karla. We are a family that will stay together through anything!

More tails . . . . Tomas, the newest one . . . .

TOMAS, THE FIRE DOG

Hi, Hi! I am **Tomas,** a Doberman/Doxie mix and I am two years old. I was rescued by Karla last year when I was a year old and couldn't be happier, except if my twin brother Casper was here with us. Casper and I were both taken to the shelter when we were one year old and waited for someone special to come along and take us home, together. But, that didn't happen. Casper got adopted after me and I went home to Karla's house. Casper and I were both skinny and sad when we were taken to the shelter and left there.

Now, I gained three pounds and love to eat, eat and eat. Once in a while, I go into the trash can by the refrigerator to see if there is anything I may want. I get fed real good by Karla and Grandpa Charlie and Matt brings me cheeseburgers once in while from work. I love them the best! (Hold the pickles and lettuce, please.)

I love to hide and play games and every day, when Karla takes off her sneakers, I flip them up in the air because I'm happy she is home and don't want her to put them on again and go out. One day, Matt and Karla came home from the movies and couldn't find me. Grandpa Charlie was out playing cards with some buddies. I was home alone. Karla and Matt looked all around for me and there I was on top of the t-v stand by the front door napping. When the door was opened, they could not see me. I was so tired that day and it took a while for me to wake up after my long walk that morning. When they found me, they laughed and called me over to them.

Another time, when they were out again, I fell asleep on the big laundry basket, under all the clothes. Karla had put the bedspreads on top of the pile, which was about three feet high and I just disappeared in the soft, cuddly bedspread. She and Grandpa laughed when they found me in the bottom of the bedspread.

I am told I am a hero too! In the middle of the night, Karla got up to take a pill and have a cigarette, (I don't approve of that) and laid down on the sofa with the cigarette. I got up when I smelled smoke coming from the sofa and Karla was not getting up. It's that darn pill, I know it. I ran to Matt's room and kept pulling on his covers to get him up. He finally did and so did Grandpa when they smelled the smoke. Karla had also got up and the house was filling with smoke. They were able to put it out and had to open all the doors for a long time. My family said I saved them and call me their "hero dog."

My family means the world to me and if I had to do it again, I would. I will always look out for them and am glad they adopted me. I think about my twin brother, Casper, and hope he has a good home like me. One day, maybe we will meet again!

Another Short tail . . . .

CHAPTER EIGHT

LOLA, THE ESCAPE ARTIST

Hello! My name is **Lola** and I am a Jack Russell and Blue Heeler mix and live in the state of Oregon with Paige, my owner and best friend.

I was found wandering on the streets alone when I was small and was brought to the Humane Society where Paige adopted me and I am glad about that. Her heart was big and caring and the following week, I went home with her and her boyfriend to her house. I was eight months old then and she gave me puppy food and water and put nice soft towels down for me to sleep on by her bed. I was happy as can be to be with someone who cared about me.

The next morning, Paige had to go to work and put me in the kitchen with a baby gate, so I wouldn't get into any trouble and stay safe until she came home from work. She put a blanket down for me to lay on by the heat and I could see out the window a little. Paige bought me this real pretty collar, black with rhinestones on it. I guess I am pretty special!

Paige has two parakeets that I really like. Their names are Rootie and Jeeter and when Paige lets them loose to fly around the house, I don't go after them or try to eat them. One time, Rootie got out the front door when a friend of Paige's knocked on the door and walked in. It happened so fast and Paige and her boyfriend and the neighbor lady across the street looked for him for hours. Paige's friend got an idea to bring out Jeeter's cage and let his calling bring Rootie back home. It worked and they got Rootie back safely before dark. Rootie had his wings cut a while ago and was not a good flyer, so Paige was very worried about getting him back.

I like to sunbathe on the windowsill in the living room, where I wait and watch for Paige to come home. When she does, we go to the park or walk the trails for a long time, especially on the weekends. Outside, I play with my toys and run around the yard.

I have a friend down the street who looks like me, but much bigger. I get excited when I see other owners walking their pets and want to play with them. Our house is on the corner, so I see everything and everybody. I get excited when Paige gets out the laundry because I know I'm going to go with her and to the park where I can run around and she tries to catch me. We have lots of fun together and I know she is my best friend.

Every day, I like to run, run and run, especially where there are open spaces, the bigger the better.

I am now one year and a six months old and have taught myself something new and that is I jump fences. My yard is fenced in and although I have enough room to run, I want to see what is on the other side of the fences. I had a friend next door, over the next yard named Meadow, a black chow dog that I used to see through the fence. I never jumped before, but one day I did not see Meadow any more and wanted to know where she was. So, I jumped my fence and the neighbor's two fences and went over to Meadow's dog house. No one was there. Her dog house was still there. Where was she?

Day after day I jumped the fence to find Meadow and she was gone. Meadow died a short time ago at the age of fourteen. She was a nice friend and I miss seeing her. I like to sit on top of Meadow's doghouse because it's so big and roomy and I can see good over the fence. Sometimes, I get loose because I jump the neighbor's fence and when the front gate is not closed, I go through it and don't know how to get back to my yard. I guess I am just a jumper and like to explore. Usually, the lady across the street finds me and brings me to my front door and tells Paige I got loose . . . . again.

I love watching the squirrels run up and down the trees in my front yard and they are so fast. Sometimes, in the summer, I get a steak bone when Paige and her friends barbeque in front of our house. Yumm! (Where's the steak sauce?)

In the winter, since my hair is short and close to my body, I get very cold if I am out too long and like to curl up on the windowsill to stay in the sunlight. I like the snow, but not being cold. I do like summer better and can stay out longer and play or go hiking with Paige. I really like the water and going rafting. I'm good at it too!

I have a new friend named Rosie who lives across the street with two other dogs. She is the one who likes me and we look at each other through our windows. She is not sure of me yet, but does comes to visit when the neighbor lady brings her over. I am happiest when I have someone to play with. I know Paige has to work, but I get so happy when she pulls up in her car and waves to me. I know she will be coming inside and spend time with me. That makes my day!

More tails . . . .

CHAPTER NINE

DUKE AND DAISEY, THE SWEETHEARTS

Howdy! Our names are **Duke** and **Daisey**. We are the proud pets of Lisa and Ricky, our friends and owners since we were one year old. Let me introduce ourselves to you. I'm Duke, a five year old greyhound and was adopted by my owner from a rescue along with Daisey, my five year old Pomeranian sweetie. We live in the big Lone Star state of Texas.

When we were adopted, Lisa was working as a Banquet Server and Ricky had a job with a real estate firm that was doing very well. All in all, life was good and couldn't be better. So, now comes the twist! Within a year, Ricky's agency was losing customers rapidly and Lisa got pregnant and was out of work for a while after her miscarriage. It was not a happy time for them or us. We really looked forward to having a brand new baby to play with and watch over. Guess it wasn't meant to be for Lisa and Ricky.

Jobs were hard to find for Ricky and he went on unemployment, while Lisa stayed home. These two people were real animal lovers and wanted to do something to help others who had animals and needed to travel or be gone for a day or two. Ricky had a dream one night about watching peoples pets at their home and bring in extra money until he got a real estate offer. In the real estate business, it was not good paying until you sold a house or business. Things got rough until then.

Lisa liked the idea too and said they would place an ad in the local paper and see what happens. Their house was big enough for a few more animals and we would be happy to have some friends too. The ad brought in a little business at first, but within six months, from referrals, business was more than they could handle. Lisa and Ricky sat down and talked about opening their own pet sitting business, but at the pet owners homes. They could do daily, weekly, vacation, sleepovers or whatever the client required.

Their first client was a single lady who worked long hours as a lawyer and had a cute little Cocker Spaniel named Cocoa. She was to be walked and fed twice a day and walked again at night. It was easy work and paid decent money. The lawyer lady referred them to other friends and business was booming. Ricky and Lisa decided that this would be their own business and see how long they could stay afloat. It was worth the try and they went ahead with their new plan.

Time went by and Lisa and Ricky split up their clients, so each dog session was filled on time and the clients were happy, as well as the pets. Summer was the best time for business as well as holidays. Ricky never wanted to return to his real estate because he loved what he was now doing so much better. There was no stress, no pitches to be made and just being happy was his mission and Lisa's. They did get out of debt within a year when they came up with an idea to bring in more business.

Since people dine out a lot and most restaurants have places for fliers and advertising is the best way to get business, they made the rounds on a slow day, if ever, and gave out brochures about their pet sitting business. It did okay, but not as well as they expected. Lisa got another idea in the middle of the night, watching a movie on t-v about a wedding. She woke Ricky up and told him they should think about getting me and Daisey married, have a dog wedding and really advertise it and invite their regular clients and new clients. Ricky jumped at the idea, (nobody asked us). It was settled. Daisey and I were to exchange howls at a wedding reception for all to see. The newspapers were notified and the radio stations and we were on our way to be fitted for a wedding gown, (not me), and a tuxedo. How silly are they!

The date and time was set for the spring and just before summer business. Invitations were sent out with our faces and two rings on the front of it. Cute, but we thought it was still silly. But, our owners needed to keep business going and we were all for that. The better the business got, the more treats and fun we got with Lisa and Ricky.

After all the planning, you know they were tired. They still had to do their regular pet sitting services and prepare for the "Big Day." My tuxedo was the regular black and white and I would not wear a top hat, no sir not me! Lisa tried but I held my ground on that one. Daisey's dress was as cute as a button and in her hair a little baby's breath on each side of her ears. She didn't like that either. A ring, (not real) was placed on a dog bone tray and brought down by Ricky to give Daisey away. The ceremony took place in the hotel Lisa once worked at.

The guests were over 75 people and the photographers were there to take our photos for the papers. We felt like real celebrities and it wasn't as bad as we thought it would be. Everyone was making a huge fuss over us and we loved the attention, until they put Daisey and me in a playpen while they ate their food. We got some new food and water in the playpen and ate, but the other food smelled better and I'll bet it tasted better too. A surprise came in the presence of Scooby Doo and he entertained the guests with a song. Bet he got tastier food that we did. And, we are the stars of this show! Lisa and Ricky did come over and bring us some doggie ice cream and we loved that. The guests had a great time and so did we and our wonderful owners, Lisa and Ricky.

Thanks to Lisa's idea that night watching t-v, it all paid off really well and we are still in business after all. Clients still talk about our "Big Day" and how wonderful the reception was. Of course, it would not have been such a big hit without the two of us. We would do it all over again to make our Lisa and Ricky happy and prosperous. They are the reason we are here with them!

Next A Long tail. . . . .

CHAPTER TEN

FREEDOM, THE HOMELESS DOG

I'm known as **Freedom,** a three year old male German Shepherd who has no home. I was given to Abby, my owner, by a neighbor friend in exchange for some crops we grew on the farm. My name of Freedom was chosen by my owner because I wander with my only friend, Abby. We used to live in New Mexico on a nice ranch and it was home for us.

Things changed for the worse for us when our ranch went into foreclosure because Abby's husband, Edgar lost all his investments from bad choices he made. They both got very sick over it and I didn't know what was happening in our house most of that time. Not only that, but Edgar got a blood clot in his leg and Abby had to take over the ranch and work at night in a diner and take care of Edgar, all at the same time. Abby was so tired most of the time and I could feel her sadness. Edgar never paid much attention to me, it was always Abby. She fed me and kept water in my bowl all the time and even though she was so exhausted, she made time for me too at night when I laid down by her feet. She would brush me and pet me and it felt so nice.

My treats got less and less as our money situation got even worse. My food was rationed to 2 cups of dry food a day instead of twice a day. I'm a big guy weighing about 100 pounds and I still felt hungry. I would get one treat a day, usually a dog biscuit. Abby would cry a lot and we would go out on the wheel swing to be alone and away from Edgar when he got mean with his words to us. Abby tried her best to make Edgar happy, but he was in such a state of depression, he didn't care.

After we had to leave our ranch in New Mexico, we didn't know what to do. Our small family lived in Canada and could not help us. We were left on our own. Edgar packed up the mini van with only our clothes and off we went to . . . where? We were scared and felt so helpless.

Abby remembered she had a cousin who lived in Kentucky and phoned him from the road on a pay phone by the gas station. Her cousin, Chet, answered the phone and Abby told him of our awful situation. Chet said he could not help us because a few years ago he had asked Edgar, who was set with money, for a small loan of $1,000. Chet had hurt his back in an accident and needed to pay his mortgage. Edgar refused. So now we are back to square one.

On the road to nowhere, we had only $900 for food and gas. Where are we going? We didn't have a clue. Abby felt if she could see her cousin Chet in person, maybe he would change his mind and soften up. Chet had become well off the last few years from the accident. Edgard had no choice but to agree to Abby's idea and we were on our way to Kentucky. At least we had some kind of destination.

We ate very little on the road, saving as much of the $900 for gas and food. We slept in parking lots and rest stops and even in hotel parking lots until we were asked to leave by a security guard making his rounds. I ate only once a day now to save the bag of dog food and make it last. Unsure of our destiny, it was a bad feeling. Tired and sad, we tried to keep each other hopeful.

When we got about 300 miles from Oklahoma, our mini van broke down with two, not one, but two flat tires that were so worn before we even started our trip. We had to use some of the remaining $621 to buy new tires which cost $129 and hurt our little bit of finances very much. There were still around 700 miles to go and didn't know if we would even make it to Abby's cousin, our last hope.

It rained heavily one day and we were glad because we could pull over and sleep in another parking lot because no one wanted to be out in the pouring rain. It was good for us because we got some needed rest and started out the next day before dawn.

Edgar had to stop when our food ran out and pulled over to a fast food place. I got a treat that day of chicken fingers. Guess Abby thought I deserved it. I did! Our water bottles got filled up with the water in the rest rooms and they even washed their faces and hands in their too. It seemed things would never get better for us.

But we finally made it to Kentucky on an eighth tank of gas. That night, we rested in an apartment parking lot and would go to see Abby's cousin Chet in the morning after some rest. I was so tired from sleeping all day in the van and was glad when we stopped so I could walk around. Abby and Edgar needed a shower badly and hoped her cousin Chet would allow them that much.

Abby made the phone call to him with fingers crossed and waited for him to answer. It rang and rang and no one picked up. Abby never knew where Chet lived, she only had his phone number, no address. They were really never that close and only kept in touch a couple times a year. Edgar pulled over to a phone booth and Abby looked into the phone book for an address that could bring her to Chet. There was no listing. Abby called most of the day and still no answer. It was looking hopeless! Chet was obviously avoiding them and they were at their wit's end.

Abby and Edgar had a choice to make. Stay in Kentucky or go back? Back to what? They filled up the mini van and drove to Missouri with $543 left. It was all they had in the world. Abby cried that night and I felt her sorrow and wondered what would happen to us. They used $49 to check into a motel and see if someone could help us. We slept like newborn babies and they showered. Boy did they feel so clean. The front desk person was rude and of no help when we asked for it.

Edgar drove into town and asked around and found a shelter that fed people. I was left in the mini van in the shade until Abby and Edgar came back. By night time, we got another cheaper motel and our money was now down to $449. Around 2:00 a.m., Edgar couldn't breathe and Abby got so scared she called the night manager of the motel who rushed right over and they called an ambulance. Abby went to the hospital with Edgar, while I stayed in the motel, alone and lonely. I missed Abby!

Abby stayed for a few hours and the hospital told her to get some rest at home (what home?) and come back in the morning. She came back to the motel and I was so happy. We went outside for a walk. Tests were taken and Edgar had suffered a mild stroke. Edgar and Abby had no medical insurance, it was canceled due to lack of payment. They knew the hospital bill would be over their heads. Oh Lord, what next?

Edgar stayed in the hospital for a week and he told Abby to save gas and come every other day, which she did. I was glad because she spent time alone with me. I liked it that way. Edgar was never my favorite person, only Abby. The motel bill for another six days came to $275,leaving us with $174. Abby was devastated and scared, so was I. One more night in the motel would leave them with only $128, their entire money, for gas, food and to survive.

A follow up check-up was ordered for Edgar a week later and he had to be at the clinic at 3:00 p.m. Abby drove him there with a half tank of gas left. Edgar told Abby not to wait, it would take a while for the check-up since there were so many people waiting. He would call her when he was done.

Abby drove back to the motel and waited for Edgar's call. It was getting late and he had not called her yet. She paced up and down, back and forth, watched t-v, ate snacks and walked me for a short while. When she came back with me, there were no messages at the front desk. By 9:00 p.m. Abby was ready to panic and phoned the hospital. She was almost out of her mind with worry. The clinic told Abby that Edgar was released and left the hospital at 5:50 p.m.

"What? I don't understand. He was supposed to phone me and he hasn't," cried Abby to the nurse.

He has to call her. Edgar has no way of getting back to the motel. Abby waited until 11:00 p.m., then phoned the police who came to the motel. Abby gave them a full description of Edgar and his scheduled appointment at the clinic and what time he had left there. Abby did not sleep all night and neither did I. She cried and cried and I moved close to her and sat by her to comfort her.

In her handbag, Abby had $128 left to her name and paid for another day at the motel, leaving $83 in her hands. She felt sick to her stomach and didn't leave the motel all day to save gas and wait to see if Edgar called her. The day manager let Abby call the police and the hospital and no word of Edgar.

Around 9:15 p.m, that evening, the night manager phoned Abby's room and said he had an envelope for her. She came quickly to the office, with me on the leash and the manager handed her the envelope. He said someone dropped it off for her around 7:00 p.m . . . that night. The night manager did not come on duty until 9:00 p.m. Who could it be from? Was Edgar hurt or even worse, kidnapped? She was afraid to open the envelope.

Abby left the office with me and sat down on the chair outside, opening the envelope. Abby nearly fainted. It was from Edgar. In the letter, he told her to go on with her life and he was making a new life for himself. He could not continue with their marriage and wished her well. (How gallant of him, the worm.) He also told Abby to sell the mini van and try to find her cousin Chet. Abby's heart just about stopped beating—it had just been shred to pieces.

I watched as she fell to her knees, crumbling up the letter in her hands. We sat on the chair outside for the longest time and Abby's tears broke my heart. Edgar had left her . . . us . . . alone in a strange town and state to fend for herself. He had abandoned us. I hate him!

Our story ends this way . . . The police came and helped us find shelter for the next day and we followed them to a car dealer who bought our used mini van for $2,500. She used most of the $2,500 for an apartment (4 months rent) and the food she got from the shelter and brought me some too.

Abby and I lost all hope for life. A few weeks later, she changed. Abby's mind must have snapped!

We now roam from place to place, calling no place home. With the clothes on her back and my dog dish in her handbag, Abby tries to take care of me before herself and she never smiles. That look is gone forever. I try to cheer her up, but it's not enough. I'm now four and one-half years old and feel lost and defeated and older than my years.

I'm tired and weary and so is Abby, but we will continue on our road to nowhere and wonder when or where it will end. I'm by Abby's side day and night and will never abandon her like Edgar did to us. Maybe one day you will see us in our travels. If so, don't judge us. This could happen to you. We never dreamed it would happen to us! Life can take a wrong turn at any crossroad.

THE END OF TEN TAILS . . . .

ABOUT THE AUTHOR

This is Maggie Tellado's fourth book and she lives in the West with her three dogs and husband. She is an avid animal lover and has rescued many animals. Her empathy for animals, especially dogs, led her to write this book to reveal, from the animal's voice, ten different stories that she hopes will touch your heart.

Maggie is a fitness person who loves to walk and hike with friends daily and enjoys being with friends and family. She is a student of Tai Chi and has studied ASL, American Sign Language from a close friend, who is hearing impaired. She loves opera and pop music and seeing plays.

Her previous books have been about womens' romance, adventure and friendships. She wants to write about different genres and expand her writing skills. Her love of writing came as a teenager, but she kept it at a low key until later in life. She feels this is the best time of her life and that writing has kept her on a steady course, hoping to write more stories for many years to come. Her many friends across the country continue to encourage her and she thanks them for their support.